YOU AND ME 9 TO 90 YEARS PART II

GAURAV PATHAK

Made with ♥ on the Notion Press Platform
www.notionpress.com

This book is dedicated to Kaira, the one who believed in me when I couldn't believe in myself. She tried to shape me into the best version of who I could be, and while I may not have reached that perfect person, every small good thing I do—no matter how insignificant—carries her essence.

She taught me more than just life lessons; she taught me how to dream, how to rise, and most importantly, how to love.

If there's anything worth celebrating in this world, it's the impact she left on me. This book is just a small tribute to her, the one who saw the potential in me before I ever did.

With the help of this book, I want to beg for her forgiveness, to apologize from the depth of my heart for all the mistakes I've made. I can only hope that, one day, she'll find it in her heart to forgive me. And if I'm lucky enough to get a second chance, my next book will be about how we reunited—how we rediscovered ourselves, and each other, with our true names.

So, Kaira, this is for you. Even if I fall short in words or actions, your presence remains in every page, every thought, and every line of this journey.

and also to my beloved father and mother, who have fulfilled my every dream, supported me unconditionally, and stood by my side through every struggle—I owe everything to you. Without your love and guidance, none of this would have been possible.

Contents

About The Author

The author of this book is Gaurav Pathak, born on 23rd June 1995 in Hazaribagh, a city in Jharkhand. He completed his schooling up to class 12th in Jaipur and then moved to Amity University, Noida, He is working in Vadodara. Presently residing in Indirapuram, Ghaziabd.

Preface

Every story is born from emotions—some of joy, some of pain, and some from the spaces in between. This book is one such journey, a heartfelt reflection of love, loss, regret, and the hope of redemption. It is not just a narrative but a piece of my soul, woven into words, shaped by real emotions and experiences.

At its core, this novel follows the story of Gautam, a man who finds himself trapped between memories of the past and the weight of his own mistakes. Through his journey, he navigates the delicate balance of longing and healing, of learning and unlearning, as he seeks solace in a world that no longer feels the same without the one he loves—Kaira.

This book is not merely a work of fiction; it is a tribute—to the people who change us, to the love that shapes us, and to the lessons we learn when we least expect them. It is dedicated to those who have ever felt the ache of missing someone, the burden of regret, and the undying hope for a second chance.

To my readers, I hope this book resonates with you in ways both big and small. If even one page, one line, or one thought stays with you, then my purpose as a writer is fulfilled.

With gratitude,
Gaurav Pathak

Acknowledgements

Writing this book has been an emotional and transformative journey, and I am deeply grateful to everyone who has played a role in shaping both this story and my life.

First and foremost, I want to express my heartfelt gratitude to my parents, whose unwavering love and support have fulfilled my every dream. Their guidance, sacrifices, and belief in me have given me the strength to pursue my passion for writing. Without them, none of this would have been possible.

To Kaira, the inspiration behind this book—thank you for teaching me the true meaning of love, resilience, and self-discovery. Your presence, whether near or far, has left an indelible mark on my soul. This book is a small tribute to the impact you've had on my life.

A special thanks to my friends and mentors, who have stood by me through thick and thin, offering encouragement, wisdom, and support at every step. Your faith in me has kept me going even in moments of doubt.

To every reader who picks up this book—thank you for taking the time to immerse yourself in this journey. If my words touch even a small part of your heart, I consider my efforts worthwhile.

Finally, to the universe, for leading me through moments of pain, joy, and self-reflection, ultimately shaping me into the person I am today.

Prologue

Some stories begin with a moment of joy. Others, with heartbreak.

This one starts with regret.

There are moments in life when we realize, too late, the value of what we had. We look back and see the missed chances, the unsaid words, the wrong turns. Gautam's story is one of those moments—a love that was once whole, a heart that was once steady, and a life that was once complete, until he lost the one person who made it all meaningful.

This is not a story of perfection; it is a story of imperfection—of mistakes that cost too much, of time that moves too fast, and of the aching hope for one more chance. As Gautam drowns in memories of Kaira, he fights against the tide of his own guilt, searching for redemption in a world that no longer feels like home.

But does love ever truly fade? Or does it linger, waiting for the right moment to return?

As you turn these pages, remember—sometimes, the greatest battles are not fought in the world outside, but within ourselves.

Let me know if you want any modifications! ?

Foreword

Literature, in its purest form, is not merely a collection of words woven into sentences, nor is it simply an assembly of narratives bound within the confines of pages. It is an experience—an alchemy of emotions, intellect, and reflection. This book, a testament to the inexorable dance between fate and free will, is not just a story; it is an odyssey through the labyrinth of human fallibility, longing, and redemption.

Gaurav Pathak, with his incisive prose and evocative storytelling, has crafted a narrative that transcends the mundane constructs of contemporary fiction. He does not merely recount events; he breathes life into them. Every word is steeped in the weight of nostalgia, every sentence echoes with the silent scream of remorse, and every chapter unfurls like a melancholic symphony composed in the solitude of a restless mind.

The protagonist, Gautam, is not just a character; he is a mirror—one that reflects the vulnerabilities we dare not acknowledge, the regrets we suppress, and the love we fail to cherish until it is reduced to a haunting memory. The interplay of past and present, the relentless pursuit of atonement, and the harrowing realization that time is an indifferent witness to human folly make this book an unrelenting emotional force.

This is not a tale of perfection, nor is it one that offers solace wrapped in comforting illusions. It is raw, it is unfiltered, and it is profoundly human. To read this book is to embark upon a journey where love is both salvation and affliction, where guilt gnaws at the marrow of the soul, and where hope, fragile yet indomitable, lingers like the final flicker of a dying candle.

Gaurav Pathak has not merely written a novel; he has etched a saga that will resonate long after the last page has been turned. For those who seek literature that does not just narrate but penetrates, that does not merely entertain but transforms—this book is an unmissable endeavor.

CHAPTER ONE

The Weight of Memories

Gautam was at a pillow shop, negotiating the price. After much back and forth, the shopkeeper finally agreed to sell it for 250 rupees. Just as the shopkeeper was about to pack it in a bag, something struck Gautam's mind. Without saying a word, he walked out of the shop empty-handed, as if a distant memory had suddenly surfaced.

He sat on his bike and glanced behind, but there was no one following him. Taking a right turn, he rode away. Along with him was his flat broker, who had accompanied him to buy essentials. The broker, a talkative man, said, "Sir, at least get a rear-view mirror installed. Someone could crash into you, and you wouldn't even know."

Gautam, lost in his thoughts, remained silent. His mind was replaying the day Kaira had first come to Indirapuram. He had developed a habit of looking at himself in the rear-view mirror, but now, its absence reminded him of something more profound—perhaps a message from fate that he was now truly alone. Kaira was no longer a part of his life. Maybe he didn't want to accept this truth; instead, he wished to continue living in the illusion that they were still together. He had learned to exist in his memories.

The broker, oblivious to Gautam's turmoil, continued, "Sir, that pillow was really good. I even got him to lower the price by 150 rupees. Why didn't you buy it? What more did you want?" Gautam wanted to answer, but he knew the broker wouldn't understand.

Instead, he decided to visit his old friend, Vivek, who was two years his senior and someone who truly understood him. Gautam rode his bike to Vivek's house. The moment they met, Gautam said, "Bhaiya, let's go home and have a beer."

Vivek smiled and replied, "Brother, I've quit drinking. But let's go eat something instead."

They went to a small eatery and ordered chow mein and paneer. Vivek, aware of Gautam's pain, simply said, "Whatever happened is in the past. Try to move on."

Gautam looked at him and replied, "I'm trying," before heading back home.

On his way, he passed a liquor shop, and right opposite, he saw the library where he and Kaira had studied together when she first moved to Indirapuram. Nostalgia gripped him. He walked into the liquor store and bought a bottle of his favorite Old Monk rum before heading back to his flat.

What was once an occasion for celebration—buying alcohol and cigarettes for a party—had now become a habit. Drinking alone was no longer an event but a way of coping. He stopped at a small shop, bought a pack of Gold Flake cigarettes, and then returned home.

Sitting in his small room, he realized the difference between drinking in a group and drinking alone. Drinking with friends was a celebration, but drinking alone only proved how broken and helpless he had become. He had brought this upon himself—his own mistakes, his own regrets.

His flat was a simple one—a small room with a folding bed, a blanket for the cold, and a bathroom. Everything was arranged just as it had been at Kaira's house, as if he was trying to recreate his past. He was on unpaid leave from work, surviving on his savings and a small income from tutoring biology. Money was sufficient, but he had learned to spend it wisely—something Kaira had taught him. He did all his household chores himself, abandoning the luxury he once enjoyed when she was around, as if he still wanted to prove to her that he could be responsible.

CHAPTER TWO

A Fading Connection

He took two glasses from the kitchen, placed them on the table, and opened his laptop. Instead of calling someone or drowning in sadness, he chose to pour his feelings into words. Writing had become his solace. He mixed the Old Monk with water, took his first sip, and by then, his laptop had booted up. It was slow, but still better than Kaira's old laptop, which she had used tirelessly for her studies without ever complaining.

As he sat there, penning down his emotions, he thought about how Kaira had spent two years without a pillow, while he couldn't even last a night without one. She used to roll up her bedsheet to make do, always insisting that she wasn't used to pillows. Just four lines into his writing, tears welled up in Gautam's eyes.

He instinctively opened Instagram and stared at Kaira's profile picture. He didn't like or comment—he just gazed at it for two whole minutes, as if she were right there with him. Her profile gave him strength. She had once given him the date of December 8th to talk, but even before that day arrived, she had called him and said, "Gautam, there's no hope for us anymore. Please move on."

He had been eager just to hear her voice, but on the other end, Kaira had become stronger than before. She had fought her battles alone. Though Gautam occasionally heard bits about her life from her roommate, he knew Kaira never shared everything—not even with her closest friends. She only revealed as much as she wanted.

Gautam stared at his phone, hoping for a call, a message—anything. He had many friends, but no one to listen to him every single day. It had always been Kaira. She would hear everything—his work troubles, his landlord issues, even the smallest details of his day. She had an endearing way of reacting, making him feel like his problems were hers too. Everyone loved talking to her for this very reason.

Now, there was no one to call. No one to tell that the Senior DPO had said something interesting today, or that his flat owner was refusing to return his security deposit.

Gautam lit a cigarette. Once, he had feared smoking because of its health risks, afraid it would harm his life. But now, he had realized something—his life partner had been much more precious than his own life. Now, he only worried about one thing—if he couldn't sleep at night, how would he get through it? If anxiety crept in, who would he talk to?

Parents are always there for support, but some emotions can only be shared with a partner. Otherwise, life feels incomplete. Gautam no longer held grand expectations for the future. He just had one hope—to see Kaira once more. Just once. If she could agree to meet him, he would cherish that moment forever, locking her image in his heart so deeply that he would never feel the need to disturb her again.

But no matter how many days passed, every ten to twelve days, a craving returned—just to see her once. Like an addict yearning for his fix, Gautam felt his world lighten for a couple of weeks just by catching a glimpse of her. But after that, the days grew heavier again.

As he finished his cigarette, the distant barking of a dog caught his attention. Irritated, he put on his earphones and played "12 Saal" by Bilal Saeed. And suddenly, a memory hit him—

That night when Kaira had gone to the terrace alone to chase away a stray dog. Gautam had been in Vadodara and was utterly confused about why she was doing that. Remembering this, Gautam ran barefoot to his terrace, opened the gate, and saw a dog with its paw stuck in the railing, looking at him helplessly.

Gautam had always been afraid of dogs, so he called the guard for help. Together, they freed the dog. Kaira's habits had now become his own—he had even started naming stray dogs. This one, after much thought, he called "Dillu." Gautam wasn't creative, so he simply modified the name from Kaira's old pet, Pillu.

CHAPTER THREE

Sleepless Nights

There were some changes in Gautam. He had started reading every message in his family group and replying to all of them—something he had never done before. The reason was simple: he had nothing else to do. He would pick up his books to study, but studying without Kaira's guidance was different. Earlier, she would help him decide how to complete each topic, structuring his study plans because his own strategies were often flawed. She had been the one to make study schedules for him, telling him exactly how to approach each chapter. Now, he missed that guidance immensely.

Gautam and Kaira had always complemented each other. He would handle the clerical work, while she was more suited for officer-level tasks. She was always the strategist, often telling him, "You can achieve something big, Gautam. You just need to stay dedicated." But now, without her, he was struggling to keep that dedication alive.

A few days ago, Gautam had visited an ashram where he met people battling their own mental struggles. He saw their pain and realized that his own suffering wasn't unique. But despite this realization, he couldn't shake off the turmoil within him. One of his closest friends from the ashram, Robin Sharma, had moved to a different city. But

Gautam, now in Delhi, decided to call him.

"Robin, how's everything going? Feeling settled now?"

Robin chuckled. "Still getting used to it, brother. And you? Still holding on to hope?"

Gautam took a deep breath. "Hope and something else—something to keep me from drowning in it."

Robin understood immediately. "Still drinking? What's the point if it doesn't help?"

Gautam laughed dryly. "It doesn't help. But it takes me back to her, at least for a little while."

Robin, curious, asked, "How does it take you back to her?"

Gautam sighed. "It's been six months now. No 'Good morning,' no 'Good night.' Just the hope that someday, I might see her message again. My mornings used to start with her 'Good morning, baby,' and my nights ended with her 'Good night, baby. I love you.' She used to get annoyed when I would send her the same message after talking to her on the phone. 'Why do you have to text it too?' she would say. But I couldn't sleep until she replied with 'Good night, I love you too.' And now? Now, my bottle of alcohol is the only thing that whispers me to sleep. In the past six months, there hasn't been a single night when Kaira didn't appear in my dreams. Sometimes, I dream that she's back, sitting next to me. Sometimes, we're riding a bike together. Other times, we're having tea, or I'm at her house, or we're walking on the streets, lost in conversation. And in those dreams, for a moment, everything feels real. The hardest part is waking up and realizing that it was all just a dream. And once I wake up, I can't sleep again."

Gautam continued, "That's why I drink. When I finally fall asleep, I want the whole world to wake up before me. Because, Robin, back in college, staying up all night used to be fun. Kaira and I would roam around Indirapuram, laughing and talking. But now, staying up at night is terrifying. It feels suffocating. I keep wondering, should I call Kaira? What would I say? 'Please, just meet me once?' And what if she refuses? What if she blocks me completely? I'm already blocked almost everywhere. The only thing left is her Instagram display picture. If I lose even that, how will I survive? That thought alone keeps me up all night."

Robin sighed and suggested, "Why don't you follow Guruji's advice from the ashram? When you can't sleep, chant 'Om' and focus on your breath."

Gautam shook his head. "That doesn't work for me. Maybe it works for you because you have no guilt. But I do. I can't even face God. It's been six months, and I haven't been able to pray. I managed to hold a puja at home once because my mother insisted, but even then, I couldn't bring myself to sit alone in front of God. How could I? I begged for a job in Baroda, and when I got it, I lost the most important person in my life. What did I trade Kaira for? A 30,000-rupee salary? I was the one at fault. My mother always warned me, 'Vinash kale vipreet buddhi'—when destruction is near, the mind stops working. She had tried to make me understand, but I didn't listen. And now, I'm paying the price."

Robin tried to console him. "What's done is done. Think about the future."

But Gautam had heard this advice from everyone. "How do I think about the future, Robin? My entire world revolved around Kaira. My mornings started with her, my nights ended with her. She was in every little moment of my day. Now, every time I try to do something, she's the first person I think of. How do I move on from that?"

Gautam didn't want Robin to know how broken he truly felt, so he forced a smile and said, "Thanks for listening, man. I'll try to sleep now."

But he knew sleep wouldn't come. He stepped outside and sat on his bed, lost in thoughts. Indirapuram, the place he once loved, now felt suffocating. He had fought with his father to buy a house here, believing he would be happy living in this city. But now, every street, every corner reminded him of Kaira. They had come here together for the first time in 2018. And now, without her, this city was unbearable.

Tears welled up in his eyes. He had bought a fishbowl—something Kaira had once used to comfort herself. When she couldn't sleep in college, she would talk to the fish, finding solace in their silent company. Gautam placed the fishbowl next to his bed, staring at it, imagining Kaira's lips forming the words, "Tough times will pass. Sleep now." He had memorized her expressions so well that he could almost hear her voice in his head.

Smiling through his tears, he pulled the blanket over himself and tried to sleep. And that night, like every night, Kaira visited him in his dreams. Sometimes, they were eating at their favorite restaurant; other times, they were having golgappas, laughing like old times.

Gautam had always slept with the lights on. But now, he turned them off. With the lights on, he could see the emptiness. In darkness, at least, he could pretend she was still there. He held onto an old green cloth—a piece of Kaira's pajama that he had taken from her scooter. It was ridiculous, he knew, but in his heart, it gave him comfort. At the ashram, Guruji had told him, "Do whatever gives you peace. If holding that cloth helps you sleep, then do it. Don't care about what others think."

And so, with the fishbowl beside him and Kaira's cloth in his hand, Gautam closed his eyes. And for a little while, he found peace in his dreams, where Kaira was still with him.

CHAPTER FOUR

Addiction with Affection

Every morning, Gautam woke up with the same hollow feeling in his chest, a weight that refused to lift. The first thing he did, almost instinctively, was pick up his phone. His fingers moved mechanically as he typed the same message he had been sending for months—"Good morning, baby." He knew the message wouldn't reach her. He was blocked. And yet, he couldn't stop himself. A single tick on WhatsApp was his only response, a cruel reminder that she was gone.

Stepping out of the house, he made his way to a familiar street corner, the one near Kaira's old apartment. He didn't walk; he just stood there, gazing at the building, at the very spot where her scooter used to be parked. Memories flooded back—how he used to wait for her downstairs, knowing exactly when she would appear with her bags: one on her shoulder filled with books and her laptop, the other carrying her lunch. He smiled bitterly, remembering the day she had to walk back alone because his phone was on silent, and he hadn't seen her call. How guilty he had felt that day. But what about now? Now, the guilt was unbearable.

He hated himself for what he had done, for letting go of the one person who made life meaningful. If someone else had hurt him, he could have blamed them. But when you destroy your own world, whom do you curse? The gods? No. He had stopped praying. The same temple where he once begged for a job in Baroda—how could he face it now, after losing Kaira in the process? He had won a job and lost his soul. Every time he tried stepping into the temple, he felt like an imposter, as if even the deity was silently asking him, "Was this worth it?"

One evening, as he passed by her apartment, he spotted the old security guard. The man recognized him instantly and stared. Gautam felt his heart clench. He had imagined this moment differently. He had dreamed of the day when he and Kaira would return together, married, bringing sweets for the same guard who had seen their love blossom. But now, all he could do was lower his gaze and walk away.

Back in his room, he shut the door and checked his phone again. Nothing. No message, no call. Just the dull ache of disappointment. He took a deep breath and opened Instagram, holding his breath as he clicked on Kaira's profile. Her display picture was still there. Relief washed over him. It was a small thing, but it mattered. As long as she didn't change it, it meant she was still there, somewhere, even if she wasn't with him.

He followed the same routine every day, like a man living in a time loop. He heated water for his bath the way Kaira had taught him—placing the rod at just the right angle in the bucket. It was such a small detail, but it connected him to her. After getting ready, he packed his lunch and walked to the same spot where he used to pick her up. If he saw a couple there, his chest tightened. He hated the way their happiness reminded him of what he had lost.

At the library, he sat at the seat Kaira once occupied. His eyes wandered, searching, hoping. Maybe someone would notice his misery, ask him to step outside for a chat. But nobody did. Everyone was busy with their own lives. He had been lucky once, blessed with a partner who had studied with him, pushed him, believed in him. And yet, he had thrown it all away. Now, he just sat there, staring at his phone, waiting for a message that would never come.

After a few hours, he stepped out, lighting a cigarette. He had never been addicted before—never needed to be. When Kaira was in his life, she had been his escape, his solace. But now, he needed something, anything, to numb the pain. As the smoke curled around him, he wondered, why hadn't he fallen into addiction yet? Maybe because deep down, he still held onto a sliver of hope. Maybe because, even through all the pain, he was still waiting for her.

And so, every night, he typed out his thoughts and sent them to Kaira on WhatsApp. He knew she wouldn't see them, but he sent them anyway. Because hope, no matter how painful, was the only thing he had left.

CHAPTER FIVE

Lost in the Echo

As Gautam returned, a sudden realization hit him—today was the day of his live test. He had been working in the Railways for a while now, but cracking the SSC exam still eluded him. Determined not to settle, he had set his sights on the PCS exams, believing that if he persevered, he would eventually break through. Since childhood, he had envisioned himself as an SDM or DSP, often saying, *"One day, I'll become a DSP, and then we'll have our own house, our own car."*

Perhaps, deep down, a part of him wanted to prove something to Kaira—that he wasn't a failure, that he had made something of himself. Even while preparing for PCS, he continued appearing for SSC exams to stay sharp and improve his command over its syllabus, particularly CSAT, which overlapped significantly with PCS exams.

Saturdays were meant for online tests, something he and Kaira used to take together. They would compare scores, their little competition fueling them. If Gautam scored higher, he would beam with pride, and Kaira would celebrate his victory with equal enthusiasm. *"You can do this! You're capable!"* she would say.

But on days when Kaira scored higher, an unspoken tension would settle within Gautam. A lingering anxiety. *If*

I can't make it, at least she will, he reassured himself. Yet, deep inside, it troubled him. Even during practice tests, Kaira would point out his mistakes, helping him improve. Her English and reasoning skills were far superior—Gautam had no doubt that she would secure a prestigious job someday.

In fact, he secretly longed for a future where Kaira's name would appear in newspapers—*Kaira Achieves Top Rank in Civil Services!* He wanted to see her success, to witness her rise in the world. That would bring him more joy than even his own accomplishments.

Their study sessions had once been sacred. But now, sitting alone, preparing for the test, he could not shake off the emptiness. He completed reasoning, math, and finally reached English. Once, he barely managed 20 out of 50 in English. But with Kaira's guidance, he had improved to 35. She always seemed more invested in his success than in her own. *She believed in me more than I did myself.*

As the test ended, he scored 142 out of 150. A personal best. Excited, he instinctively took a photo of the result, opened WhatsApp, and hesitated. Whom could he share it with? Without thinking, he sent it to Kaira's blocked number with a simple message:

"The score is good this time. I'll aim for even better next time."

He knew she wouldn't see it. But sending it still felt like a ritual he wasn't ready to let go of.

After the test, they used to go for long walks, discussing everything from philosophy to career plans. Now, Gautam wandered the streets alone. He saw couples sharing meals, laughing, lost in their world. *That could have been us.*

A familiar ache settled in his chest as he unlocked his phone, scrolling through old chats and photos. One particular image caught his eye—Kaira, standing outside the library gate, leaning against her bike, smiling. A moment frozen in time.

He exhaled deeply, lost in memories. *Life is long, but what should I do with it? What goal should I chase now?*

The clock struck 8 PM. Once, at this hour, Kaira would nudge him—*"Let's go. Time to pack up."* But tonight, no one was there to say those words. He could leave whenever he wanted, yet the freedom felt hollow.

Restless, he stepped outside and lit a cigarette. The nicotine barely calmed his nerves. He searched for distractions—NGOs, old-age homes, something, anything—but nothing filled the void.

As he turned back to the library, his eyes fell on the whiteboard where Kaira used to jot down motivational quotes. It had been wiped clean, yet faint traces of her handwriting remained. His heart pounded. His vision blurred. He traced the faded ink with his fingers, as if touching it would bring her back.

A sudden rush of emotions overwhelmed him. He staggered outside, gasping for air. He sat on the stairs, then on his bike, then back to the stairs—unable to decide what to do. His mind screamed for escape.

He started his bike and sped towards home, parking outside without the strength to enter. Instead, he dialed his father's number.

Talking to his father always made him feel secure, as if nothing could go wrong. Tonight, he needed that assurance more than ever. He spoke about mundane things—his job, his studies—stretching the conversation as long as he could.

"You're doing well, son. Keep going," his father said.

After a long silence, Gautam finally whispered, *"Okay, I'll call you later."*

He knew he couldn't burden his family with his struggles. *How long can I keep making them a part of my pain?*

His parents still thought he was in Baroda, working, unaware that he had taken unpaid leave and moved to Delhi for preparation. He had kept them in the dark because he knew they would worry.

But nothing was working. The weight of regret crushed him.

Unable to bear it any longer, he grabbed his bag and left again. He found himself at the tea stall outside Gate 3—Kaira's favorite place for morning tea. The vendor recognized him.

"One tea, less sugar," Gautam muttered.

The vendor handed him the cup and asked, *"Who are you waiting for? Your bike's right there."*

Gautam blinked. His head spun.

Had he just imagined Kaira's presence?

A cold shiver ran through him. He gulped down the tea and rushed back to his rented room. He couldn't take it anymore. If this was how life was going to be, he wasn't sure he wanted to continue.

Lying on the bed, he clutched an empty bottle of Old Monk. His mind raced—flashes of Kaira's teary eyes, her voice, her absence. He tried watching YouTube videos, scrolling endlessly, distracting himself.

Nothing helped.

He thought of the antidepressants a doctor had once prescribed. They lay untouched in his drawer. He never took them, afraid of becoming dependent on them.

But tonight, everything felt unbearable.

He reached for the bottle, only to find it empty.

He stared at the ceiling. Then at the aquarium. He dipped his fingers in the water, watching the fish swim away, detached from his pain.

"If this is how it's going to be... let it all end tonight."

The thought lingered.

CHAPTER SIX

A Call at Midnight

Gautam was lost in his thoughts, unsure of what to do next when suddenly, a memory resurfaced. He recalled meeting a Bengali girl at the ashram while practicing yoga. She was around 24 years old—married at 22, but she had lost her husband in a tragic accident. After his death, her in-laws refused to keep her, and even her own family shut their doors on her. Her father had already passed away, and her elder brother and sister-in-law also refused to take her in. Helpless and abandoned, she took up a job as a teacher in a small school, earning just enough to survive.

She had come from a small town in Rajasthan and had likely come to the ashram for the same reason as Gautam.

At 10:30 PM that night, Gautam dialed her number. She answered hesitantly, "At this hour? Is everything okay?"

Their previous conversation at the ashram had left an impact on him. Talking to her, he had felt an unspoken sadness—her pain was unjustified, yet she endured it. Maybe that's why, at this moment, he saw a reflection of Kaira in her suffering.

But the difference was striking. This girl had lost her husband to fate, to death—something beyond anyone's control. But Kaira? She had been betrayed. *Losing someone to fate is painful, but losing them to deceit is unbearable.*

He asked her a simple yet deeply personal question:

"When your husband left, how did you manage everything alone?"

There was silence for a moment. Then, she chuckled softly, as if amused by the question. "Situations make you strong. You learn to manage everything on your own," she replied.

That was all Gautam needed to hear.

He wasn't trying to compare their pain—he was trying to understand Kaira's. When he wasn't there, how did she manage everything alone? He had heard from someone that Kaira hadn't been keeping well, that she had been visiting doctors alone. She had some digestive issues, making it difficult for her to eat properly.

He remembered seeing her once, riding her scooter alone, going to get medicine. She had no one. She had to take care of herself, both physically and emotionally. And now, that thought was tormenting him.

He had called the Bengali girl not just to talk but to confess—to admit the weight of his guilt. But what she told him next shattered him even more.

She recounted the day she was thrown out of her home—her in-laws had literally pushed her out. In the chaos, her phone slipped from her hands and shattered on the stairs. She had no way to contact anyone, no money, no support. She had begged them, saying, *"Just get my phone fixed so I can call my brother. Buy me a ticket so I can go home."* But no one listened.

Hearing this, Gautam felt the ground beneath him collapse.

It struck him that he had done something far worse to Kaira. This girl had been abandoned by society, by fate. But Kaira? She had been abandoned by him—the person who was supposed to love her the most.

Maybe he had called to seek redemption. Maybe he wanted someone to tell him he wasn't a terrible person. But instead, the conversation only magnified his sins.

He had once told this Bengali girl, *"Think of me as your elder brother. If you ever need help, let me know."* And yet, he had been the very reason for someone else's pain—pain much deeper than what this girl had suffered.

His hands trembled as he held the phone. His entire body felt numb. His mind flashed back to Kaira, to her anxiety attacks, to the nights she had spent crying.

In a desperate, guilt-ridden outburst, he spoke into the phone, *"You think I'm a good person? You think the people who hurt you were bad? No, I'm worse than them. Worse than your in-laws. Worse than anyone you've met. You call me your brother, but I am the most disgusting, vile creature you could ever know. I don't even deserve to be your brother! Stay away from me! Just stay away!"*

The girl on the other end was stunned. She had no idea what had triggered this. Before she could respond, Gautam ended the call.

She tried calling back, but he had already blocked her.

Gautam sat there, suffocating under the weight of his own words. It was as if he had just admitted, for the first time, the full extent of his crime.

His breath grew heavier. His heartbeat pounded in his ears. He was spiraling.

His mind screamed, *I can't live like this. I can't bear this anymore.*

He wanted to call Kaira. He wanted to beg for forgiveness, to tell her how much he missed her. But he knew she had blocked him. If he sent a message, she might block him there too. And the thought of losing even that last sliver of connection stopped him.

He crawled under his bed, curling into the darkness. His mind raced with one thought—*I need to get out of this. I need to escape. I can't do this anymore.*

But this world is cruel. You don't get to leave when you want. You don't get to decide your exit.

Time passed. It was 2 AM. The sound of passing trains echoed in the night.

With no other option left, he grabbed his bike and sped to **Nizamuddin Railway Station**—the same place where he and Kaira had once boarded the train to Baroda.

The station was crowded, buzzing with movement even at that hour. He found an empty bench and sat down, pulling his jacket tightly around him. He had brought a blanket, knowing he would spend the night there.

He closed his eyes and began chanting under his breath.

"Om Namah Shivaya... Jai Bajrangbali... Om Namah Shivaya..."

For someone who had once felt ashamed to face God, he now had no one else left to turn to.

The night passed in restless murmurs, his mind seeking peace where none existed.

And as the first light of dawn broke through the sky, Gautam sat there—just another lost soul in a city that never stopped moving.

CHAPTER SEVEN

Echoes of Her Presence

As the first rays of the sun touched the horizon, Gautam felt a sense of relief—finally, the night had passed. Stepping out of the railway station, he made his way to a public washroom, freshened up, and decided to head home. The previous night, he had left in such haste that he had neither taken his phone, wallet, nor bike keys. He had no recollection of how he had covered a twelve-kilometer distance, walking continuously from 2:00 AM to 3:30 AM, only to reach the railway station.

After arriving home, he quickly grabbed his bag and headed straight to the library, determined to begin his studies for the day. Upon entering, he noticed two people arguing inside. Initially, he had no interest in their quarrel, but then he overheard the girl say, “So, just because you came in first, does that mean I shouldn’t enter at all?”

Gautam’s mind had begun associating every girl in distress with Kaira. Without hesitation, he turned toward them and asked, “What happened?”

The guy looked at him and scoffed, “Why are you interfering, bro?”

Gautam, already filled with pent-up anger, stared at him and firmly replied, "Because I will." The guy hesitated for a moment before speaking again.

The girl explained, "He walked into the girls' washroom and used it, leaving it in such a condition that no one else could use it after him."

The guy immediately defended himself, "Madam, didn't you see the sign outside? The boys' washroom is under maintenance. Where else was I supposed to go? And when I went in, you weren't even there!"

The girl interrupted, "Will you let me finish?"

She continued, "When I went inside, he had used the washroom in such an inconsiderate way that it was impossible for anyone else to use it properly."

The guy, still defensive, retorted, "How else do you use a washroom? You want to teach me?"

That was the breaking point for Gautam. He grabbed the guy's hand and said, "Let me teach you then. This is a toilet seat. When you use it while standing, you must lift the seat. And when a girl needs to use it, she can lower it and sit without any mess. Do you even know the kinds of infections that can spread if you don't?"

Gautam's voice carried an authority he himself hadn't known before. He was never someone who prided himself on his actions, but Kaira had tried hard to make him a better person. And while he was improving, something inside him had also become bitter—something that made him react strongly to situations like these.

The girl looked at Gautam, somewhat surprised by his intense reaction. But Gautam wasn't thinking about her; he was lost in his own world, convinced that if any girl suffered injustice, it was as if Kaira herself was being wronged. If Kaira had taught him something and it wasn't being followed, then it was a grave mistake. His perception had been shaped entirely by her influence.

Just then, the library owner arrived and diffused the situation. "Alright, don't create a scene. I'll make sure the other washroom is fixed soon," he assured them.

Gautam nodded. "Good. Girls come here to study, not to catch infections," he said before walking away and settling into his seat to begin studying again.

His focus was now on becoming a PCS officer, aiming for DSP or SDM positions. He remembered the first time he had started practicing with Kiran Publications' 9600-question book, solving it multiple times with Kaira's help. But now, he was struggling with Laxmikanth's *Indian Polity* because the library was always crowded during lunchtime, and there weren't enough seats. Though earlier, he would study with Kaira by his side, now he sat alone, eating lunch beside his bike, staring at it in silence.

After lunch, he followed his usual routine—buying a cigarette, smoking it outside, and returning to study. He had once enjoyed riding around Indirapuram with his friends, but now, even when he stepped outside, it was only when something caught his attention. That day, he noticed smoke rising in the distance.

"Where is that fire coming from?" he muttered and instinctively ran towards it. His mind had been conditioned to react as if Kaira herself was driving a fire truck to extinguish it. When he reached the location, it turned out to be something minor, and he walked back, aimlessly wandering before finally returning to the library.

By the time evening arrived, Gautam felt emotionally drained. It was Sunday, a day when his father usually stayed home. Sundays used to be special—they would take the car and drive around with Kaira. But now, nothing felt the same.

Feeling a rare craving for good food, he went to a street vendor and ordered a bowl of noodle soup. But the moment he took the first bite, memories flooded his mind—Kaira cooking for him, making all his favorite dishes, from noodles to cheese omelets. He remembered how rare it was for him to cook anything, yet she had always managed everything alone.

His heart ached. He clenched his fists and muttered under his breath, "Kaira, please, just forgive me once. Give me one chance to make things right. I promise I'll never make a mistake again. Just come back, please."

But no one heard him. He left the soup untouched and walked away, heading back to the library to pack his books and bag before returning home.

Back at home, he instinctively looked at the painting Kaira had gifted him. It reminded him of their trip to Soil Village for a painting camp—how she always painted when she was upset. He tried watching something on Amazon Prime but ended up rewatching *Panchayat*, recalling how he and Kaira had laughed together watching it. He replayed the final scene multiple times, but this time, he wasn't laughing—he was remembering her laughter.

Kaira's brother had a friend who was a social media influencer. Gautam began following her stories religiously, hoping to catch a glimpse of Kaira. A couple of times, he did, and those moments gave him a strange sense of joy. But when three days passed without any new stories, his anxiety spiked.

By midnight, Gautam's anxiety was unbearable. To the world, it had been seven months since their breakup, but for him, it felt like it had just happened. His wounds hadn't healed—they had only deepened. Others had moved on, but he was still stuck in the past, burdened by guilt and longing.

At 11:30 PM, he poured himself two drinks of Old Monk, took his anxiety medication, and scrolled through random articles about redemption, second chances, and how people atone for their mistakes. At one point, he even read that serving at an old-age home for seven days could bring peace. He had tried that too—but nothing changed.

Kaira had loved animals, and for a brief moment, Gautam considered getting a pet cat, just like they once had with Rancho. Maybe, he thought, taking care of a cat would make him feel like he was doing something for her, even if she was gone.

That night, he followed his usual ritual—checking Kaira's profile, staring at an old photo, and searching for any unread messages or emails from her. There were none.

Eventually, sleep overtook him, but only after drowning in the memories of a love he had lost.

CHAPTER EIGHT

Another morning, another day, another hope—would she come today?

Gautam left his house and headed towards the library. As he moved forward, something crossed his mind, and he suddenly stopped. He parked his bike by the roadside and noticed a temple. It was the same temple he often visited when he prayed for a job.

Inside the temple, there was an old sage with a long beard, a true ascetic. Gautam felt a strange connection with him, as if the sage could reveal something about his future. Once, when he was desperately praying for a job, the sage had blessed him with a banana. After Gautam ate it, the sage placed his hand on his head and said, "You will get what you seek very soon."

A few months later, Gautam secured a job.

This temple was special to him, and he had even brought Kaira here once. However, Kaira didn't like it. The presence of smoking sadhus and the smell of marijuana made her uncomfortable. But Gautam had always felt a deep attachment to the place, believing it held some divine power for him.

As he walked past the temple, he saw the sage on the road. Without a second thought, he ran to him and fell at his feet.

"Baba, I got what I wanted... but in the process, I lost something precious. I have committed a grave sin."

The sage lifted Gautam, placed his hand on his head, and said, "Your suffering will end soon. But the path to your happiness will be difficult. You must pass a tough test."

Hearing this, Gautam's face lit up. *Maybe... maybe Kaira is coming back into my life!*

Excitedly, he asked, "Baba, tell me something, anything... When? How? What should I do? I am ready for anything!"

The sage smiled. "It is not about what you do. Just focus on doing good deeds, and she will come back to you on her own."

These words sent Gautam into a frenzy of joy. He ran ahead, his heart filled with new hope.

Life was throwing unexpected twists at him, but he knew one thing—he could not plead to God for forgiveness. He had wronged someone deeply.

After some time, he reached the library. As he opened a book, the librarian approached him.

"Bhaiya, didi used to come here often."

Gautam froze. "Wh—who? Kaira?"

"Yes, she used to visit regularly after you left. She seemed lonely... just wandering around."

Tears welled up in Gautam's eyes. He couldn't bear it. Without saying another word, he grabbed his phone and pretended to take a call, rushing out in embarrassment.

He kept replaying the librarian's words in his head. *Kaira was suffering... while I was drowning in my own filth.*

Gautam's guilt consumed him. He wandered aimlessly until he noticed a poster for an NGO. He approached a volunteer and asked how he could join.

"You can speak to our founder," the volunteer replied.

Gautam called the number immediately.

"Sir, I want to join your organization."

"What do you do?"

"I'm a government employee in the Railways, currently on unpaid leave. I'm preparing for PCS exams and also want to do something meaningful."

"That's great! You can start from this weekend."

Gautam had found a purpose. The NGO worked with underprivileged children—exactly what Kaira was passionate about.

Kaira had always wanted to help orphaned kids by providing them with education. Now, Gautam made it his mission.

The NGO couldn't pay him much, but he didn't care. He asked for just ₹100 per class, only to use that money to buy books for the kids.

For the first time in months, he felt like he had a direction.

But deep down, he knew that another long, sleepless night awaited him

CHAPTER NINE

A Mirror to Pain

The same morning once again. As Gautam woke up, the first thing he did, out of sheer habit, was to pick up his phone and send a message— "Good morning, baby"— to Kaira's blocked number. It had been four months now, yet he could not move past August. Each morning, his fingers instinctively followed the same ritual, as though tethered to an invisible chain of longing.

After sending the message, he got up and began getting ready for the day. As he dressed, a sudden, piercing scream reached his ears. Alarmed, Gautam rushed outside, locking his door behind him. On the street, he saw a woman struggling to hold her little child while wailing in distress. Without a moment's hesitation, he sprinted towards her.

"Didi, what happened? Are you alright?" he asked urgently, offering her a bottle of water. The woman could barely speak; her lips trembled, and her exhausted eyes mirrored a sorrow that words could not articulate. Her child, too young to comprehend the gravity of the situation, clung to her tightly, his innocent gaze flickering between his mother and the concerned stranger.

Gautam knelt down and gently inquired, "Beta, what happened to your mother?" Before the child could respond, the woman, gathering whatever strength she had left, gasped, "Do you have a phone? Please, I need a phone."

Gautam wasted no time. He guided them toward his home, but the woman hesitated, unwilling to step inside. Sensing her apprehension, he quickly fetched a chair from his study table and placed it outside for her. For the child, he found a small plastic stool.

"Please sit," he urged. "Should I bring you something to eat?"

She shook her head firmly. "No, I don't need anything."

There was a haunted emptiness in her voice, a kind of emptiness that carried the weight of shattered hopes. Gautam, now deeply concerned, pressed on gently, "Tell me what happened. Maybe I can help."

The woman hesitated, her fingers clenching the fabric of her saree. Then, in a voice thick with grief, she began, "My husband came here six months ago to work. We stayed behind in the village. I brought my son here so we could be with him, so we could be a family again. I thought... I thought he must be struggling, working tirelessly to make ends meet. I wanted to surprise him, to cook for him, to care for him. But..."

Her voice broke, and tears streamed down her face. Gautam felt a lump rise in his throat. He did not know her pain, but he recognized it. He had seen it before—within himself.

"What happened next?" he asked softly, though his heart already knew the answer.

She swallowed hard and continued, "When I reached the place where he lived, another woman opened the door. I—I didn't understand at first. And then... then I saw my husband behind her, looking at me as if I were a stranger."

She could not go on. Sobbing, she buried her face in her hands.

Gautam sat still, unable to move. The scene played out in his mind, but instead of this woman, he saw Kaira. He saw himself standing where her husband had stood. A slow, suffocating realization dawned upon him. He had done the same.

A wave of panic surged through him. His breath quickened, his hands trembled. Without warning, he gripped his own head, as if trying to physically hold himself together, and gasped, "I made a mistake... I made a terrible mistake... Please forgive me. Give me one more chance. Just one chance. I swear, I will never do this again. I love you... I love you more than anything... Please, forgive me..."

The woman, startled by his sudden outburst, recoiled slightly. People on the street had begun to stare. A few whispered among themselves, exchanging puzzled glances.

"What are you saying?" she asked, confusion and unease flickering in her tear-streaked eyes.

But Gautam was no longer speaking to her. He was speaking to someone who wasn't there. He was speaking to Kaira.

"I was wrong," he murmured, his voice barely above a whisper. "I was blind. I left the only person who truly loved me. I was selfish, foolish... I thought I had everything, but I had nothing... Nothing without her..."

The woman's son tugged at her hand, watching Gautam with wide, curious eyes. But the mother only sighed and shook her head. "Men are all the same," she muttered bitterly. "Heartless creatures. You throw away love like it means nothing and then beg for forgiveness when it's too late. You are no different. You are filth."

Gautam did not argue. He did not try to defend himself. He only whispered, "You're right. I am filth. But please... please, just one chance..."

He ran inside, grabbed his phone, and thrust it towards her. "Call your brother," he insisted. "Tell him to come here. You don't have to go anywhere. You don't have to worry. I will not let anything happen to you. Just stay here until he arrives."

The woman hesitated.

"Please," he added, his voice desperate. "You and your son can sit here. I will lock my door from the outside. I will not come near you. You are safe. Just wait for him here."

Still wary, she took the phone and dialed the number. Her hands shook as she held it to her ear. Gautam, watching her, felt an overwhelming sense of helplessness.

A little later, her brother arrived. He took one look at Gautam and, with open hostility, snapped, "We don't need your help. Keep it to yourself."

Gautam took a step back, his body still trembling from the weight of his emotions. He wanted to say something, to explain, but the words never came.

A few minutes later, the woman's husband's mother was called. Her response on the phone was chillingly indifferent:

"So what? Let her die if she wants. What's the bigdeal? A man is free to do as he pleases."

Gautam's control finally snapped. He grabbed the phone and shouted, "If it were your son dying, would you say the same thing? If he were betrayed, abandoned, would you be this indifferent?"

The woman's brother placed a firm hand on Gautam's shoulder and murmured, "Let it go, brother. This is not your fight."

But Gautam could not let it go. Not when he saw his own sins reflected before him, not when the universe was forcing him to witness the pain he had once inflicted. He stepped back, overwhelmed, and locked himself in his room.

And then, he broke.

Collapsing to the floor, he sobbed uncontrollably. Guilt, regret, despair—they clawed at him, suffocating him. Time lost all meaning. Hours passed, but he remained there, drowning in his own torment.

Somewhere in the depths of his agony, a name surfaced in his mind.

Dr. M.K. Jain.

Kaira had mentioned him once—a psychiatrist she had visited. Gautam had even consulted him telephonically. So he like his walk of handling things. With whatever strength remained in him, he called a Rapido and set out to find the doctor who might be his only salvation.

CHAPTER TEN

The Revelation

Gautam sat waiting for Dr. Jain for a long time. After some time, Dr. Jain entered the room. Gautam's eyes were swollen, he had been crying all day and was consumed by his own pain. As soon as Gautam saw Dr. Jain, he stood up from his seat. Dr. Jain, with a smile, greeted him, "Come in, Gautam, sit down. Tell me, what's troubling you?"

Gautam looked at Dr. Jain, smiled faintly, and said, "Sir, you already know all my troubles." Dr. Jain, a little puzzled, replied, "I don't quite understand. How could I possibly know? This is our first meeting."

Gautam looked at him and said, "No, Sir. We've spoken before over the phone, and I've met you once before as well."

Dr. Jain, a bit confused, asked, "When? I don't remember."

Gautam looked at him quietly for a moment and then replied, "I understand, Sir. You meet so many patients, it's not possible to remember each one of them. But I'm sure you remember the girl named Kaira who came to you between July 18th and 20th. She was heartbroken because her fiancé had betrayed her, and she was devastated."

Dr. Jain's expression shifted as he recalled the incident. "Yes, I remember Kaira. She came to me because her fiancé from Baroda had betrayed her. She was very upset."

Gautam smiled weakly and said, "Yes, Sir. And I'm the one who caused all this. I'm the reason she's suffering."

Dr. Jain observed Gautam's face closely and knew that this man was in deep emotional turmoil. Gautam appeared broken, and it was clear that he was seeking help for something far deeper than just physical pain. Dr. Jain, sensing his distress, offered, "Would you like some tea, coffee, or water?"

Gautam, feeling vulnerable, asked, "How long do you usually spend with your patients, Dr. Jain?"

Dr. Jain chuckled softly. "Well, Gautam, I'm a professional, and my time is dedicated to solving your problems. Typically, I allot half an hour to each patient, but I'm here for you as long as it takes to help you."

Gautam, desperate for more time, immediately handed over double the regular fee and said, "I need at least an hour of your time, Doctor."

Dr. Jain smiled and said, "Of course, Gautam. You can take up my full hour. Now, tell me everything."

Gautam took a deep breath and began, "Sir, there was a girl named Kaira who came to you between July 18th and 20th. Her fiancé had betrayed her, and she was in a lot of emotional pain. She felt shattered, and I know she was in deep distress when she came to you."

Dr. Jain nodded, acknowledging the situation. "Yes, I remember. Kaira was struggling a lot. Her fiancé from Baroda had let her down. She was devastated."

Gautam continued, "And I am the one who caused all her pain. I am the one who drove her into that state of heartbreak."

Dr. Jain, understanding Gautam's guilt, replied, "I do remember you. You called me after Kaira's visit. You asked me to speak to her and help her understand her situation better. I remember you even paid for my consultation to help her. But, Gautam, I only made one call. And that's when you say things went wrong. You believe I could have done more, but remember, I'm a doctor, not a relationship counselor. My job is to heal the pain, not fix relationships."

Gautam lowered his gaze, his voice filled with sorrow, "Sir, I understand, but I feel like I failed her. I think if you had called her just one more time, maybe she wouldn't have felt so alone. She needed someone, but you only called her once and left it at that."

Dr. Jain, with a calm demeanor, replied, "Gautam, I'm a doctor. I help people manage their physical and emotional pain, but I'm not here to intervene in their personal relationships. I can't take sides or fix what's broken between people. It's not my place."

Gautam sat quietly, reflecting on the doctor's words. He knew deep down that the doctor was right. But the weight of his guilt was overwhelming, and he was struggling to let go of the idea that somehow, Kaira's pain was something he could have fixed if only he had done more.

Dr. Jain looked at him with empathy and said, "You've come here seeking answers, Gautam. The truth is, you can't change the past, but you can learn from it. Kaira's journey is her own, and you need to focus on your own healing now."

Gautam nodded slowly, his heart heavy. "I understand, Sir. Thank you for your time."

Dr. Jain looked at Gautam and said, “Now, tell me, what's going on? You seem more troubled than before. How can I help you? It's been six months since you've been stuck on this issue. Why are you still stuck in the same place?”

Gautam forced a smile and replied, “Sir, even if it were sixty years instead of six months, I'd still be stuck. My final destination lies somewhere else. But I haven't reached it yet."

Before Gautam could say anything more, Dr. Jain interrupted. He looked at him and said, "Where were you that day? You speak of 60 years, but that day, when you were forming a wrong connection with someone else, you already had a good, understanding, and decent girl like Kaira. And yet, you ruined everything for her. You only called her once, right?"

Gautam could sense Dr. Jain wasn't happy with his approach, and perhaps the therapist within Dr. Jain was trying to speak, trying to point out Gautam's mistakes. But instead, Dr. Jain remained quiet and instead became more of a friend. Gautam, trying to lighten the mood, responded with a laugh, "Sir, I don't even remember that day. That's why I'm suffering now. I'm dying inside."

Dr. Jain, as if understanding everything, nodded and said, "You were acting one way at the airport, and when you went to Kaira's house early in the morning, but at night when you went to kaira's brother's place your intentions were different. Now, suddenly, what's happened? Why is love overflowing for her all of a sudden?"

Gautam lowered his eyes and replied, "Sir, for the past seven months, I am saying this at airport and at her house in morning , I beleived I nned a person to stay but with within sometime I realised that without Kaira I can't even survive peacefully for a second. What do you want me to do? Did you come here to ask for the money I gave you earlier? Or are you going to tell me again that you couldn't help me convince Kaira? You couldn't fix my mistakes, right?"

Dr. Jain stayed silent for a moment, as if pondering his response. Then Gautam looked up and, with a serious tone, said, "Sir, I didn't come here to get the money back. I didn't come to complain. My situation is not good. Every night, I sleep like it's my last night. I feel like tonight will be the heaviest night of my life. I need your help, Sir. Someone spoke to me about you, and now I'm here. Please, listen to me one last time, and don't turn me away."

Dr. Jain looked at Gautam, and in a calm voice, he asked, "How can I help you?"

Gautam, now with a pleading expression, said, "Please, don't turn me down. I really need someone to listen to me right now."

Dr. Jain was visibly angry and irritated by Gautam's words, but deep down, his inner doctor was telling him repeatedly, *"Please, treat him. Help him."* Still, Gautam seemed to be stuck in his own world, consumed by his emotions.

Gautam, desperate to make his point, spoke again. "Sir, that girl came alone. A guy from the radio station came for her too, and he stayed by the gate until late. At least, you could've stepped outside to check if she left safely or not."

As Gautam continued speaking, he shifted the blame back onto Dr. Jain. The constant accusations made Dr. Jain lose his temper. After hearing this, Dr. Jain, who had been observing patients since morning, became furious with Gautam. He abruptly said, "Maybe I should quit my practice and dedicate myself to helping you. You seem to need that more than anything right now!"

The truth was, Dr. Jain knew exactly what kind of person Gautam was, and that made his irritation grow. He could see through Gautam's facade and was aware of his true nature. Despite his frustration, Dr. Jain found himself puzzled as he looked into Gautam's eyes, which reflected a deep, inexplicable helplessness.

Gautam, noticing Dr. Jain's silence, chuckled awkwardly and said, "I'll only start your treatment under one condition, Gautam. You have to answer a few of my questions first." He continued without waiting for a response, "My first question is, when you were involved with another girl in Vadodara, did you think Kaira's love for you was still intact? Was her love still there when you were with someone else?"

Before Dr. Jain could even pause to see Gautam's reaction, he answered immediately, "Sir, Kaira was always in my mind. I was with that girl, but my conversations with her started casually. She asked me, 'Do you have a girlfriend?' And that's when everything started to fall apart. For the first time in my life, I tried to hide Kaira's existence from someone. I told her, 'Yes, I'm single.'

What happened next was even worse. In my mind, there was a criminal voice telling me, '*You might only be with this girl for a month, and after that, you can walk away. No one will know. No one will care.*' But I won't say that now. Before, I was loyal. I'd never been in a situation like this before. Everyone is loyal until they get a chance to cheat."

Gautam's voice softened, almost regretful. "But with Kaira, it was different. She never looked at another guy in that way. She never gave anyone a chance. To make sure she wouldn't feel bad, I even turned down an offer from an old school friend who wanted to meet me on a scooter ride. I knew that if she saw me with another guy, she wouldn't like it."

He paused, as if he had to gather his thoughts before speaking again. His voice trembled as he said, "But still, despite all of that, I was a disgrace in her life. Even though she was loyal to me, I thought about cheating on her. I thought, '*It's just one month. No one will know. What harm can it do?'* I never realized how wrong I was until now."

Gautam's words hung in the air, heavy with guilt and self-loathing. There was a rawness in his tone, a recognition of his failure. He had betrayed Kaira's trust, and now he was dealing with the consequences—his own pain, his inner torment.

Dr. Jain sat silently, his expression unreadable, absorbing everything Gautam had confessed. The weight of the situation was starting to settle in.

Dr. Jain's questions continued to pierce through the layers of Gautam's mind, each one revealing more about his internal struggle. The air in the room was heavy with guilt, and Gautam's voice shook as he responded to the next question.

Dr. Jain leaned forward, his gaze intense as he asked, "So now tell me, why were you texting that girl when Kaira was running away from your house? You were in trauma, struggling with the fear of loneliness, and you were afraid Kaira might never come back to you. Is that true?"

Gautam's face twisted with the pain of the memory. "Yes, Sir. I was afraid of being alone. Kaira had always been a part of my life, and I couldn't bear the thought of losing her. It was as though the world would collapse around me. I had gotten so used to her presence, I couldn't imagine a single second without her. I was terrified that Kaira would never expect me back into her life."

He paused, struggling to breathe, his eyes welling up with emotion. "And so, I thought... I thought maybe the girl from Vadodara would help me fight this loneliness. I tried to distract myself. I knew I was wrong, but in that moment, I couldn't see any other way out."

Dr. Jain, sensing something deeper, interrupted, "So, this is the same reason you acted that way at the airport too?"

Gautam looked down, his voice barely audible. "Yes, Sir. I tried my best to stop Kaira from leaving, but when it became clear that she was walking away, I was consumed by the fear of being alone. And then, in my desperation, I turned to the girl from Vadodara. I thought... if Kaira wasn't with me, maybe this other girl would stay, maybe it would fill the emptiness. It was the second worst mistake of my life. I was thinking about myself, not about her, or anyone else. I only thought of my own fear of solitude."

He took a shaky breath before continuing. "But in that moment, I realized how selfish I was. I knew I was hurting Kaira. And I couldn't live with that. I wanted my punishment for my mistakes, but I needed Kaira to stay with me. Without her, I felt incomplete."

Dr. Jain observed Gautam in silence, his expression hard to read. After a moment, he asked the next question. "Alright, Gautam. Let me ask you this: after you met her at the house—after she called you that night—you were okay the entire night. But what happened the next morning? Why did you act the way you did?"

Gautam's face twisted in pain as he recalled that day. "I thought I had Kaira back. But when the girl from Vadodara called in the morning, I felt like I needed to clear things up with her. She said something that made me think... maybe Kaira wasn't ready to accept me again. She was still in denial, still hurt. I asked her again, 'Please, Kaira. Accept me,' but she wouldn't. And in that moment, I thought about myself again. I thought maybe the girl from Vadodara could stay in my life. Maybe she could fill the void that Kaira was leaving behind."

His voice faltered. "But as I was walking down the stairs, everything from our time together in Indirapuram came flooding back. I remembered how we used to live, how happy we were. Kaira's smile—everything about her meant the world to me. And now, I was the reason for her tears. I couldn't control it. I knew I had to fix it, no matter what."

Tears started to well up in Gautam's eyes, and his voice broke. "I ran to my mom and asked for help, hoping that I could somehow fix this. But by the time I reached Kaira, it was too late. She was already about to leave with her brother. Watching her walk away, tears streaming down her face... was the worst feeling I've ever experienced. The guilt crushed me."

Gautam's voice was barely above a whisper as he continued. "Since that day, I've been calling the girl from Vadodara, begging her to forgive me. I've told her that we can't be together. I don't deserve her. I've been fighting to get Kaira back, enduring all the suffering I deserve. I just want Kaira back, Sir. I need her."

As Gautam spoke, his emotions broke free. He placed his hands on the table, hiding his face in them as he wept uncontrollably, tears staining the table in front of him. Dr. Jain sat quietly, watching the outpour of raw emotion, understanding that Gautam had finally acknowledged the depth of his pain.

CHAPTER ELEVEN

The Broken Pieces

The room was thick with silence as Gautam sat, tears streaming down his face uncontrollably. His pain was evident in every sob, every tremble that ran through his body. Dr. Jain sat there, watching this man fall apart before him, and for the first time since their conversation began, he felt something stir inside him—his inner doctor, his ability to empathize and understand.

Dr. Jain's stern expression softened as he watched Gautam. The frustration and irritation he had felt earlier slowly melted away, replaced by the realization that Gautam's agony wasn't about a momentary mistake, but about the wreckage of his heart. He understood now why he had been asking all those tough questions—why Gautam had been struggling to accept his own actions, his own flaws, and why Kaira, the one person he loved, was slipping further away from him. Dr. Jain leaned forward, his voice gentle, yet firm.

"Gautam," he said, his tone filled with an underlying compassion, "listen to me now. You've been living with fear. You've been running from your own self. Before you can do anything, you need to face that fear."

Gautam barely looked up, his voice barely above a whisper. "Sir... since June 23rd, I knew... I knew Kaira was the one. I couldn't stay with anyone else, not for even a second. It felt like I couldn't breathe if she wasn't around. Kaira... she's my life. Without her, I might as well die alone. But I never thought I'd have to lose her like this. Now, I know, if I can't have her, I'll stay single for the rest of my life, hoping that one day, at some twist in time, she'll come back to me. I deserve to suffer for everything I did. But believe me, Sir, if I can get Kaira back, I'll bear all the pain—every single ounce of it."

Dr. Jain listened closely, his eyes scanning Gautam's face, taking in every word. He could feel the weight of Gautam's emotions, the desperation that clung to him like a shadow. He could see that Gautam wasn't just crying for the loss of Kaira—he was crying because he knew he had caused her pain, and he couldn't forgive himself for it. He knew the journey ahead wouldn't be easy for Gautam, but something about his sincerity, his regret, made Dr. Jain feel that he could find redemption.

Then, Dr. Jain asked the question that had been lingering in his mind for a while. "Gautam, one thing's been bothering me. When you were in Vadodara, and Kaira saw you with someone else, you didn't shed a single tear. Your eyes were dry, and yet now, you're crying like this. Isn't that a bit of a double standard?"

Gautam's eyes snapped upward as he met Dr. Jain's gaze. His heart clenched at the question, but he knew he needed to answer honestly.

"Sir, at that time," Gautam began, his voice shaky, "I didn't know what to do. I didn't cry because Kaira was with me till the time she is with me, I can sleep walk eat in a proper way but the time she is away from me everything feel devasted. In front of Kaira I know I committed a crime but if she is with me. i have the full power to fight with my inner soul and bring it back to a track by making it suffer.

Dr. Jain's brow furrowed. "So, you're telling me you'd go to any lengths to fix this. But how far would you go to get Kaira back? What's your limit?"

Gautam didn't hesitate, his voice full of determination and sincerity. "There is no limit, Sir. I'll do anything. I'll never harass her. I'll wait for as long as it takes. From a distance, I'll do whatever I can, but I'll never force her. If she decides to come back to me, I'll be ready. But if not, I'll wait, patiently. I won't pressure her, but I'll wait."

Dr. Jain looked at him for a long moment, measuring the gravity of his words. "Anything? Even if it means giving up everything you have?"

Gautam nodded, his voice resolute. "Yes, even that. Sir, if there's a patient who needs a kidney transplant, I'm willing to give mine. I'll do it without asking for anything in return, without money. Maybe through someone else's blessings, I'll save someone's life—but I need Kaira back. That's all I want."

The rawness in Gautam's voice, the depth of his regret, and his willingness to sacrifice everything—these things shook Dr. Jain to his core. He knew Gautam was speaking from a place of deep sorrow, but also from a place of redemption. He could see the shift, the change that was taking place inside him.

Dr. Jain took a deep breath, his eyes softening as he spoke. "Gautam, you've made mistakes, but you're not beyond redemption. You're struggling with your own demons, and you need to face them. You need to rebuild the trust that was broken—not just with Kaira, but with yourself. You're going to have to fight, but you have to do it the right way. The pain you're feeling now—use it to make you stronger, to help you become the man you know you can be. But remember, no one can force someone to love them. You'll have to earn Kaira's trust again. And if she's meant to be with you, she will come back. But you can't rush it. You can't control it."

Gautam nodded, wiping his tears, his resolve strengthening with every word Dr. Jain spoke. For the first time, he understood that the path to redemption was not going to be easy. He couldn't take shortcuts. But if he truly wanted Kaira back, he had to change—inside and out. He had to prove that he was worthy of her love.

Dr. Jain sat back, watching Gautam, seeing the conflict in his eyes. "This is your journey now. The road ahead will be hard, but you've taken the first step. Now, all you have to do is keep moving forward."

Gautam gave a faint, bittersweet smile, finally feeling like he might have a chance—just a small one—but a chance nonetheless. "Thank you, Sir. I won't stop. I'll keep fighting for Kaira. I promise."

CHAPTER TWELVE

The Weight of Silence and Despair

The past two to three days had passed in a haze of normalcy, but deep down, Gautam couldn't escape the restlessness that gnawed at him. Another sleepless night crept upon him, his mind consumed by thoughts of Kaira. He found himself endlessly waiting for messages or updates, hoping to catch a glimpse of her presence in some small way. Each notification, each message from her was a lifeline—a connection that brought him some semblance of peace. Without it, he felt lost, adrift in a world that seemed colder and more distant.

If more than three or four days passed without hearing from her, Gautam spiraled. His mind would race, searching for ways to fill the void, ways to survive the hollow days. It was as though his entire existence hinged on these tiny, fleeting moments of contact. Without them, Gautam began to question the very meaning of his life, wondering how he could keep going without her presence.

In these moments of longing, Gautam became increasingly disillusioned with the society around him. He felt a deep sense of disdain for the world, particularly when he encountered any form of negativity or cruelty. It was as if every evil he saw in others mirrored something within himself. He began to see his own reflection in the flaws of those around him. The things he had done, the choices he had made, seemed to have marked him. The weight of his past mistakes began to weigh heavily on him, affecting him in ways he hadn't anticipated. It was a deep, almost unbearable shame that took root inside him.

The air in Delhi had turned bitterly cold, a sharp contrast to the warmth that Gautam so desperately craved. The chill pierced through his skin, sending shivers down his spine. He couldn't help but think of Kaira, who always felt the cold so intensely. He remembered how, in the library, she would wear two or three sweaters to shield herself from the biting cold. She would wrap herself up, not just to stay warm, but to keep the chill at bay, to fight the discomfort that seemed to follow her everywhere. Her feets get cold so quickly so she puts on three pair of leg in order to keep it warmer

Gautam could almost feel the cold winds as they whipped around him. Every gust of air seemed like a message from Kaira herself, a silent plea for help. "It's too cold," he imagined her saying. "I can't study. I can't focus." The thought of her being in pain, even from something as simple as the cold, filled Gautam with a profound sense of helplessness. He wished, with every fiber of his being, that he could be there for her, to wrap her in warmth and offer her comfort. But he wasn't there. He wasn't by her side. And that realization crushed him.

The cold winds that seemed to touch him wherever he went felt almost like a constant reminder. Each gust whispered cruelly in his ear, "Kaira is better off without you. She's better off having left a fool like you behind. It's you who will suffer now. You deserve this emptiness."

The voices in his head grew louder, more unforgiving. The isolation he felt without Kaira's presence became a suffocating weight on his chest.

It had now been 7 or 8 days without any word from Kaira. Each day that passed without any update from her only deepened his sense of anxiety and despair. Gautam felt as though he was slipping into a dark, all-encompassing void. The emptiness around him mirrored the emptiness inside. Without Kaira's messages, without her presence in his life, he felt more and more like a shell of the person he once was. The once vibrant spark that Kaira had ignited within him seemed to flicker and fade with every passing day.

His thoughts grew darker, spiraling into a state of deterioration. The world felt unbearably heavy, and Gautam wasn't sure how much longer he could carry it. His connection to Kaira, which had once been a source of hope and joy, now seemed like a distant memory. Every day that passed without hearing from her made it feel more and more like a cruel, heart-wrenching reality. Gautam couldn't help but wonder if he was losing himself in the process, if the pain of not having her in his life would eventually consume him entirely.

In these moments of isolation and despair, Gautam found himself at a crossroads. The uncertainty of his future without Kaira felt unbearable. But even in the midst of his suffering, there was a small part of him that still clung to the hope of reconnecting, of finding a way to break free from the darkness and into the light once more. But the days without her, the silence, seemed to stretch on forever. Each second without her felt like an eternity.

Gautam was beginning to wonder if he'd ever find a way out of the spiral he had fallen into

CHAPTER THIRTEEN

The Crossroads of Guilt and Redemption

Whenever Gautam was overwhelmed by anxiety, he sought out different ways to relieve his inner turmoil. A glimpse of Kaira or even a simple message from her for just a few minutes was enough to give him a sense of peace. But when days turned into weeks, and he received no word from her, his mind spiraled into a pit of unbearable pain. The absence of her presence seemed to tear him apart. It felt as though his very existence depended on hearing from her—if he didn't get the comfort of her updates, the weight of uncertainty crushed him.

In this emotional chaos, Gautam found himself caught in a cycle of fear and hesitation. He feared reaching out to Kaira, terrified that if he did, and she didn't reply, it would be a devastating blow that might push him over the edge. The thought of rejection paralyzed him, leaving him in a constant state of emotional paralysis.

He felt disconnected from the world around him. His guilt over past mistakes consumed him so completely that he couldn't bring himself to visit a temple. His shame for his actions, for the pain he had caused Kaira, felt like a weight too heavy to bear. It was as if the level of his transgression made him unworthy of stepping foot in a place of worship. The inner conflict gnawed at him, leaving him feeling trapped between his desire for redemption and the overwhelming guilt he carried.

One evening, around 9 p.m., Gautam stood at the gate of the temple. His mind was a storm of emotions, and he wasn't sure what he was seeking, but something inside urged him to be there. He hesitated at the entrance, unsure if he should step inside. Just then, the Sandhu Baba, who had once offered him a banana before his selection, called out to him from within the temple. He waved Gautam over and offered him a banana as prasad.

Gautam looked into the Baba's eyes, and for a moment, a strange connection passed between them. Though there were other people sitting around, Gautam felt an urge to speak, but words failed him. He had met the Baba a few days earlier outside the library, and the Baba had recognized his face. With a kind gesture, the Baba asked Gautam to sit with him. Despite his anxiety, Gautam took a seat, though his body trembled.

The silence stretched on, and for the next 15 to 20 minutes, Gautam and the Baba sat in quiet companionship. People began to leave one by one, and eventually, it was just the two of them in the temple. Gautam's heart raced, his thoughts swirling as he waited for the Baba to speak, to offer some kind of guidance or relief. All Gautam wanted was to share his burden, to speak his truth. He hoped that the Baba's presence would offer some kind of solace, some way to ease the weight in his heart.

Finally, the Baba broke the silence, looking at Gautam with deep, knowing eyes. "Tere taklif kya hai?" he asked gently. Gautam had been waiting for this moment, for someone to acknowledge his pain and allow him to speak.

He felt a rush of relief, and for the first time in days, he was ready to open up.

With a heavy heart, Gautam began to speak. "Baba, I met you outside the library the other day..." he started, but before he could continue, the Baba interrupted him in a stern tone, "Yaad nahi mujhe. Jo bhi hai, fir se bolna hai toh bol, nahi toh rehne de."

Gautam felt a pang of guilt but quickly apologized. "Baba, I've made a mistake. I've hurt my future wife. I deceived her because of another girl..." He lowered his gaze, unable to look the Baba in the eyes as he confessed the depth of his wrongdoings.

The Baba's gaze hardened as he looked at Gautam. "Chup karne waala toh Kansa aur Ravan se bhi badha raksha hai," he said sharply. His words stung, and Gautam felt the full weight of his guilt settle deeper in his chest.

Gautam tried to explain himself, his voice trembling. "I know, Baba. I am ashamed. But I feel so lost. I'm tormented by what I've done." The Baba's eyes softened for a moment, but his words were still harsh. "Tu sharminda hai? Aur us bechari ladki—Kaira ki baat kar rahe ho? Uske saath itna bada afradh karte hue tujhe sharam nahi aayi? Kitne dukh mein hogi wo. Kiss tarike se tarap rahi hogi wo. Aur tujhe bas apne dukh ki padi hai?"

Gautam's heart broke as the Baba's words hit him like a thunderclap. He felt the crushing weight of his actions. He hadn't truly understood the depth of Kaira's pain until now. The realization struck him with a painful clarity.

"I want to make it right, Baba. I'll do whatever it takes. I want to fix this," Gautam said, desperation in his voice. "Whatever service I can do, I'm ready."

The Baba, still observing Gautam closely, fixed him with a stern look. "If you really loved Kaira, how could this have happened? If you loved her, this wouldn't be possible. Why did you do it?" The question hung in the air, and Gautam felt the full force of his regret. He swallowed hard, trying to find the right words.

He looked at the Baba, his voice barely a whisper. "Baba, there was this one thought in my mind... I thought I couldn't live without Kaira. But somewhere along the way, I got distracted. I let attraction cloud my judgment. It wasn't love... it was a fleeting desire. I made a terrible mistake. But my love for Kaira, that's real. It's selfless. I can't love anyone else like I love her."

The Baba's expression hardened once again, his patience wearing thin. "Nikal ja yahaan se," he snapped. But Gautam, his resolve firm, refused to move. He stood his ground, repeating his words in a desperate plea. "If you want to, you can throw me out, but don't send me away from here. I need to stay. I need to fix this."

The Baba's gaze bore into him, but Gautam wouldn't budge. He clung to his hope, despite the Baba's anger, despite his own shame. He wasn't leaving until he had made peace with his mistakes, until he found a way to make things right with Kaira, no matter how hard the path ahead would be.

And so, in the quiet of the temple, amidst the silence and the weight of his guilt, Gautam stood resolute, hoping for a chance at redemption, hoping for a way back to Kaira's heart.

CHAPTER FOURTEEN

A Struggle for Redemption

As Gautam stood before the Baba, he could see that there was no love or affection in the old man's eyes. The Baba had no personal attachment to Gautam, but there was a quiet respect in his gaze, born out of his years of experience in understanding human struggles. Gautam's persistence was undeniable, and despite the Baba's stern exterior, he decided to listen. But in his heart, the Baba also knew that Gautam was battling with his own selfishness—a selfishness that was tangled up with his desire for peace and his need to atone.

Baba finally spoke, his voice filled with curiosity. "Toh tu kya karne aaya hai?" he asked, his tone flat but heavy. Gautam, without missing a beat, answered with unwavering honesty, "Mujhe har jagah, har mod par, Kaira ka ek presence chahiye. Jahan bhi uski yaadon ki ek chingari ho, wahi meri zindagi ka raasta hai. Woh yahaan thi, aur ab main yahaan hoon, sirf uski yaadon ke liye. Jab yahaan rehta hoon toh aisa lagta hai ki main uski yaadon mein jee raha hoon, aur inhi yaadon mein so raha hoon. Mera dil bas chahta hai ki main in yaadon mein kho jaaun."

The Baba looked at him with a piercing gaze, studying him as if trying to read the layers of his pain. "Tere maa-baap kaha rehte hain?" he asked, as though searching for some grounding in Gautam's life.

Gautam answered, his voice tinged with a sense of detachment, "Woh log ab Jaipur mein rehte hain. Main yahaan ek room rent par le kar rehta hoon, aur main waise hi rehta hoon jaise Kaira yahaan rehti thi. Har chiz wahi karta hoon jo Kaira karti thi. Grapes mein dahi daal kar bhi khata hoon..." He chuckled faintly at his own absurdity, the irony of his actions not lost on him. But it wasn't enough to mask the deep sorrow in his heart.

Baba's eyes narrowed, and his tone shifted from curiosity to something more forceful. "Apni kaam par dhyaan kyu nahi deta? Apni zimmedariyon se bhag kyu raha hai?" he asked sternly, as if trying to shake Gautam from his numbness.

Gautam, defensive yet resolute, responded quickly, "Nahi, Baba. Main kahiin bhi nahi bhaga hoon. Main leave without pay ki permission le kar yahaan aaya hoon, aur ab yahaan hoon, bas Kaira ke saath."

The Baba raised an eyebrow, clearly frustrated by Gautam's lack of focus on his duties and responsibilities. "Tu apni yaadon mein kho kar samajh pe kyu nahi dhyaan deta? Pehle bhi ek bhojh tha, aaj bhi utna hi bada bhojh hai," Baba said with growing irritation.

Gautam, already overwhelmed by the gravity of his guilt, felt a sharp pang in his chest. "Baba, ab main ek NGO mein padhta hoon. Agar yahaan mandir mein koi seva ho mere layak, toh main apne dil se usse karna chahta hoon," Gautam said, a desperate hope tinged in his voice.

The Baba's gaze softened for a moment, but his words carried the weight of wisdom. He fixed Gautam with a gaze that seemed to pierce into his soul. "Pehle apne paap ka kaam kar. Uske baad yahaan aane ka sochna. Yeh ek pavitra mandir hai," the Baba advised, his voice calm but firm.

Gautam, overcome by a mix of guilt and exhaustion, nodded. His heart felt heavier than ever, burdened not just by his mistakes, but by the realization that he had to change before he could ever hope to find peace. As the words sank in, Gautam's body and mind gave in to the weariness that had been building inside him for days. Slowly, his eyes began to close, and in the quiet of the temple, Gautam fell asleep, caught between the yearning for redemption and the deep ache of his own sorrow.

In that moment, Gautam realized that his journey to make amends was only just beginning, and that true redemption would only come when he faced the consequences of his actions and worked to rebuild the life he had shattered. But for now, sleep offered him a brief respite, a moment of stillness before the storm of his emotions would rise again.

CHAPTER FIFTEEN

A Heart Torn, A Soul Searching

It was around 2:00 AM the next day when Gautam woke up. He noticed that Baba was still smoking something, his face etched with anger. Gautam tried to ask him about it, but a sense of fear held him back, and he closed his eyes again. Suddenly, Baba shouted at him, "Wake up! You're sleeping again. When she was here, she stayed awake, crying, while you kept snoring away! You were lost in your sleep, and now, now you still can't wake up, sinner."

Gautam hadn't told Baba about what had happened, but the harshness of his words struck him deeply. He quickly sat up in bed, his mind racing. "How do you know all this? How do you know what happened between us?" he asked in disbelief.

Baba looked at Gautam, his gaze piercing. "There are things we don't need to explain. You don't always have to tell us everything. But you should understand, Gautam, that we know more than you think. Before you even speak, we already know."

Gautam, overwhelmed, could only stare at Baba. "But Baba, after everything I did to her, after all the mistakes I made, I don't even know what to do now. She said she's happier without me, and I can't even find the courage to tell her that I want her back. What should I do?"

Baba chuckled softly, his tone surprisingly gentle. "At least you understand that much. That's a start. But tell me, what do you want now?"

Gautam, on the verge of tears, replied, "I just want her in my life, Baba. I want to live with the memory of her. As long as I can feel her presence, even from afar, I will be content. I don't need anything else. When I was with her, even for just eight days, I felt like the happiest man alive. And now, I burn with the pain of missing her every single day."

Baba, amused, picked up a walnut from the table and began trying to crack it open. Gautam watched as Baba broke it with ease. Then Baba handed him a second walnut, and they both pressed them together, the shells cracking open with a satisfying snap.

Gautam couldn't help but smile. It was a quiet, shared moment between them, filled with an unspoken understanding. He remembered the time when he had asked Kaira how she cracked walnuts, and she had told him, "My father is an engineer; he taught me how to do it."

The memory made him smile again, and the laughter between them felt healing.

Suddenly, Baba's hand rested gently on Gautam's head, and he spoke in a softer voice. "You miss her terribly, don't you?"

Tears welled up in Gautam's eyes, and he whispered, "Yes, Baba. I can't live without her. Every day, I wait for her messages, for her calls. I love her so much, Baba. I just... I just want her back in my life."

Baba's voice turned serious. "So, why do you stay in Indirapuram, Gautam? What is it about this place?"

Gautam paused for a moment, then replied with a heavy heart, "This is where we shared so many memories, Baba. Every road, every corner here reminds me of her. We used to drive around this city at night, on her scooter, together. Everything here... everything is connected to her. That's why I want to stay here. It's the only way I can hold on to her."

Baba, sensing Gautam's pain, asked, "But what about your work? Are you not doing anything for a living? Are you not burdening your parents?"

Gautam quickly answered, "With your blessings, Baba, I got a job last year, in March 2024. I work in Vadodara, but honestly, I don't know if it's going well. I took unpaid leave from January 16, 2025. Since then, I've been staying here at my brother's place, living with him. My quarter is locked up, and I'm just living in one room with a washroom. I'm managing with that."

Baba raised an eyebrow. "But if you're living here, Gautam, your salary must have stopped, right?"

Gautam nodded, then continued, "Yes, Baba. But Kaira used to teach tuitions when she was here. She gave all her earnings to me—she never kept anything for herself. Right now, I've saved up about ₹30,000, but she won't take it back. If I try, she just blocks me. I don't know what to do, Baba."

Baba's face softened, but he still cautioned, "You're scared, aren't you? Scared of losing her. But Gautam, if you had been honest with her, if you hadn't played with her heart, things might have been different. Remember, she came to your city, left everything behind to be with you. She was there for your birthday, and yet you hurt her. How do you think she felt when she discovered what you did?"

Gautam, tortured by guilt, cried out in agony. "Baba, I can't bear it anymore. I'm dying inside. I don't know how she managed to survive it. How did she live with that betrayal? She never even told me what she was going through."

Baba paused for a moment before responding, "Have you ever wondered how much pain she must have been in? She had her own struggles, Gautam. She never burdened you with them, but she had her own battles. And you... you betrayed her trust. You hurt her deeply, Gautam. And now, you want her back. But remember, there's no guarantee that she'll return."

Gautam, now in tears, whispered, "I don't deserve her, Baba. But I will wait for her. I will wait for her to come back into my life."

Baba nodded, his voice firm but kind. "Never force her, Gautam. Wait, but don't pressure her. Your good actions, your sincere prayers, will guide her back to you, if it's meant to be. But if she doesn't come, you must learn to live with that, too. Don't keep hoping for what might never be."

Gautam, filled with remorse but determined, nodded slowly. "I won't pressure her, Baba. I will wait. If it's meant to be, it will be."

Baba's expression softened even more. "And if you find someone else, Gautam, remember this: once you've loved someone as deeply as you love Kaira, no one else can take their place. You must stay true to her memory, for she was the one who truly mattered."

Gautam bowed his head. "I've made mistakes, Baba. But now, I want nothing more than to honor her memory. She will always be the one I love."

Baba placed his hand on Gautam's shoulder, giving him a final word of wisdom. "The pain you feel now is the price of your actions. But if one day, your heart truly repents, if you're worthy of forgiveness, then perhaps, just maybe, God will grant you a second chance. But until then, focus on your deeds, your actions, and never forget the lessons you've learned. If she comes back, cherish her with all your heart. And if not, live with the strength to move on."

Gautam, filled with a bittersweet sense of clarity, wiped his tears and nodded silently. He knew this was the only path forward—no matter how painful it might be.

CHAPTER SIXTEEN

Memories in the Dark

The morning was quiet when Gautam found himself sitting alone in his room, lost in his thoughts. His mind wandered back to the time when he was with Kaira. In those days, there was a confidence within him that he had never known before. But now, that same confidence had shattered, and he felt like a broken man. No longer able to look anyone in the eye, unable to speak to anyone, he withdrew from the world around him, hoping that something good might happen. Perhaps today, or maybe tomorrow, something would change. He clung to the faint hope that things might work out someday, even though he couldn't see a clear path ahead.

Lost in these thoughts, he suddenly had an idea: *Why not watch a movie?* It had been so long since he had seen one, and the last time he had watched movies, it was with Kaira. Every moment with her seemed tied to something beautiful. He had never watched a movie without her by his side. But as the thought of watching a film came to his mind, he remembered the movie *Sultan*, where Salman Khan and Anushka Sharma's characters go through a separation. He remembered the deep sadness in Salman Khan's eyes when he was alone, and how, in the end, Anushka Sharma's character returned to him. Gautam watched that scene again and again, feeling a strange connection. It made him wonder if there was hope for him, too, that maybe, just maybe, Kaira might come back one day.

Gautam had been living in Indirapuram, and despite the geographical distance, he felt closer to Kaira. In his mind, her house was just down the street, as if they were separated by only a few steps. In reality, though, the distance between them was vast—around 30 kilometers. But he didn't care about the distance. He held on to the thought that she lived just around the corner. Perhaps if he stayed patient, something would bring them together again. He opened his phone and put on *Sultan*, watching intently as the scene played out in front of him.

As the movie continued, Gautam couldn't help but feel a strange sense of hope building inside him. He imagined himself, just like Salman Khan's character, fighting for a second chance. He longed for the opportunity to show Kaira how much he loved her, how deeply he regretted the mistakes he had made. But he also realized that just like in the movie, there were no guarantees. He didn't know if Kaira would come back, but watching *Sultan* gave him a strange sense of solace, even if it was fleeting.

Gautam's thoughts drifted back to another film, *Sanam Teri Kasam*, which Kaira had once shared with him. It was a South Indian movie starring Naga Chaitanya, and they had watched it together online during the lockdown. It had been a special time for them—an escape from the world, where they were simply two people sharing a quiet, beautiful moment. They had watched the movie together, each from their own homes, but feeling so connected. At one point, they both began calling each other during the movie, asking how far along they were, sharing their thoughts about the scenes. It became the best movie-watching experience Gautam had ever had.

Gautam smiled at the memory. He remembered how Kaira had always been so dedicated when it came to watching movies. She couldn't bear any distractions, always wanting to immerse herself fully in the experience. Gautam would sometimes get distracted, wanting to talk to her during a scene, but she would scold him, saying, "If you're going to talk, don't watch with me!" Her dedication and love for the films they watched together had always impressed him.

As he watched *Sanam Teri Kasam* again, Gautam couldn't help but feel a deep sense of inadequacy. The loyalty and love of the male lead, so true and pure, made Gautam feel small in comparison. He couldn't even finish the movie; the emotions overwhelmed him. His eyes filled with tears, and he realized that his love for Kaira had always been real, but his actions had betrayed her. He couldn't undo the past, but he wanted to make things right. He longed for the chance to rebuild everything, to earn her forgiveness, if only she would come back into his life.

Whenever the weight of his regret became too much, Gautam would go to the metro station, the place where he and Kaira had once met. The stairs where she used to come down to meet him—those memories were like a balm for his broken heart. He would sit there, watching people pass by, imagining that Kaira was still walking down those same steps toward him. He would think about the times they had gone for tea together, sitting at their favorite spot at Yadav Tea Stall in Indirapuram. The little moments they shared, like buying tea and drinking it together while sitting at the metro station steps, were memories he clung to.

The place was now more than just a station—it was a shrine to his memories with her, a place where he could still feel her presence, even though she was no longer there. Gautam missed those simple moments. He longed for the day when, just like before, she would walk down those stairs and call him, asking to share a cup of tea, just one more time.

CHAPTER SEVENTEEN

The Weight of Regret and Redemption

Gautam, in this chapter, is grappling with the overwhelming sense of loneliness and confusion that clouds his life. Though surrounded by a sense of failure, he finds solace in the comforting calls from his father, who has always been a source of motivation for him. His father, a man of wisdom and patience, knows more than Gautam thinks about his life and mistakes. While Gautam often tries to dodge reality with his little white lies, his father, despite being upset with him, continues to guide him toward the right path.

The conversations between father and son in this chapter reveal the deep bond they share, even though it's strained at times due to Gautam's past actions. Gautam reflects on his life choices, particularly the shortcuts he's taken and the lies he's told, which have only complicated his journey. His father tells him that there's no easy way out of mistakes—only the hard work of correcting them and not repeating them. Despite the tension, Gautam feels reassured by his father's words, understanding that no matter how many mistakes he's made, his father will always be there to help him.

This chapter also delves into the relationship Gautam had with Kaira, his partner in life and work. Their bond, based on mutual respect and shared dreams, contrasts with Gautam's impulsive decisions and regrets. His father advises him to not dwell on the past mistakes with Kaira but instead to work toward redemption by motivating Kaira to pursue her dreams and reach her full potential, even if they are not directly communicating anymore. The subtle but clear message is that Gautam must not let his own guilt or failure prevent Kaira from reaching her goals.

Gautam sat quietly, lost in his thoughts, the weight of his past mistakes pressing on his chest. He had agreed with the wisdom his father had shared with him; yet, as much as he understood the importance of making amends, a selfish thought lingered at the back of his mind. The hope of Kaira returning to his life was enough to keep his heart beating, but it wasn't just about her coming back. It wasn't only about mending what was broken between them. He wanted something more—something beyond reconciliation.

In the depths of his heart, he longed for Kaira's success. Not just any success, but the kind of success that would make her name shine brightly in the world. He wanted to see her in the newspapers, hear about her achievements on the radio, see her on TV. Kaira was not just the girl he loved; she was the embodiment of everything he felt he had lost. In some strange, desperate way, he wanted to prove to the world that she was everything he couldn't have—everything that he had, in his own foolishness, let slip through his fingers.

Was this a selfish motive? Perhaps. He couldn't deny it. But in his desperation, it was the only thing that kept him going, the only thing that gave him a glimmer of hope. He thought that if Kaira could rise to extraordinary heights, maybe he could find some sense of peace, knowing that she was living her life to the fullest. He envisioned her success as his own, as though the fruits of her labor might somehow fill the emptiness inside him.

But it wasn't just about pushing Kaira toward greatness for his own sake. No, it was deeper than that. He knew that she deserved it. He knew that she had it in her—the brilliance, the potential, the fire. He had seen it in her every step of the way, and it hurt him to think that his own mistakes might have been the reason she was now distant from him. And so, in his mind, he made a plan. He would do whatever it took to help Kaira realize her extraordinary potential. Even if it meant stepping back, even if it meant putting his own desires aside, he would push her. Push her beyond limits, beyond what she ever thought was possible.

As for Gautam himself, he felt the need to do something more for his own redemption, something that would at least give him a sense of purpose, a reason to live without the constant burden of guilt. He decided that he would work for an NGO, adopt children, and devote his life to giving them the love and care they deserved. By doing so, perhaps he could lift the weight of his own failures from his heart. Maybe, just maybe, in the act of caring for others, he would find a way to heal the broken pieces of himself.

But there was more. In the quiet moments of his service, in the days spent helping children who had no one else, he would feel Kaira's presence. He would feel it in the smile of a child who found comfort in his care, in the hope of a life made better through his actions. Through his work, he would feel like he was sharing a part of her—her compassion, her kindness, her drive to make the world a better place. He wanted to live in that space, where he could not only make amends for his past but also feel

Kaira's essence in the extraordinary work he was doing.

And so, Gautam moved forward with a determination that burned in his chest, a combination of love, guilt, hope, and the desperate need for redemption. He knew that no matter how many times he stumbled or how many mistakes he made, as long as Kaira's name continued to shine, as long as she achieved greatness, he would find a way to keep pushing forward—both for her and for himself.

CHAPTER EIGHTEEN

Letters to Kaira

Gautam was lost in his thoughts, caught between the past and the present. A cloud of regret loomed over him, and he felt the intense need to express everything that weighed on his heart. So, he thought about writing to Kaira—a letter that might not reach her but would, in some way, set him free. But to find the courage to do so, he needed something to break through his own hesitations.

He remembered an old habit, a fleeting escape from reality. He had a couple of puffs of marijuana from an auto driver—an instant connection to a different world. As the smoke clouded his mind, everything felt lighter, almost surreal. He closed his eyes, and it was as if Kaira was right next to him, her presence comforting and real.

With the haze clouding his thoughts and the intoxication taking over, Gautam began writing. The letter started with something familiar, something tender:

Dear Chotu,

Good morning, Baby. Mere chotu sa baby abhi bhi so raha hai, plz uth jao na... Thik hai, mai 30 mins mein uthatha hu aapko.

After 30 minutes...

Chotu Baba, uth jao!

Imagining Kaira's reply, as if she were lying right there, sleeping, Gautam grinned.

Huhhh... uth gaya hu mai...

It was a simple message, a playful interaction, yet it held a depth of emotion that only he could feel. He was trying to imagine Kaira's response, as though she were still a part of his world, and somehow, that brought him peace.

His mind wandered as he continued, the words flowing onto the paper, as if the high opened up a window to his soul. Gautam began describing memories he had with Kaira, the small moments that meant so much to him. He remembered the little things—like how they would meet at the library before grabbing coffee, how he would try to impress her with his small acts of kindness, how they would laugh over the tiniest jokes. Everything he wrote felt like a lifeline to a time when things were simpler, when Kaira was his.

He told her about a government vehicle photo he had found online, a vehicle given to someone from New Zealand's Ministry of External Affairs. Gautam wanted to show Kaira that even small achievements mattered. He wanted her to know that if she could reach great heights, so could he. He was determined to prove to her that he could better himself too.

In his writing, he began to recall moments when they were together—like when they had lunch together, and he would make a joke about how he left no crumbs on his plate. He imagined Kaira laughing and calling him a "good boy." Or when they went to DMart, where Gautam tried to convince Kaira to buy healthy food, and in that moment, he even tried to buy a juice for himself. At the checkout, the bill came to 800, but Gautam, in his anxiousness, told the cashier it was only 600. He immediately realized his mistake and told Kaira, *"Mai kabhi jhoot nahi bolunga."* He laughed at himself, feeling ashamed but relieved in some way.

The vivid memories continued to flood his mind. He remembered taking Kaira to the swimming pool in his society, floating with her in the water, and calling her "Kanahiya." It was playful, innocent, and full of warmth. Gautam imagined Kaira replying lovingly, "Swimming pool mein mai chotu hu, Kanahiya toh bahar hu na..."

The day felt like a whirlwind of memories, moments he wished could be relived. But Gautam knew that he had made mistakes. And now, as the high began to fade, he felt an overwhelming urge to ask for forgiveness.

As they sat at the café, enjoying shakes together, Gautam couldn't hold back any longer. He looked into Kaira's eyes, his hand reaching for hers.

"Kaira... mujhe ek mauka de do," Gautam said, his voice desperate. *"Main apni puri zindagi tumhare saath jeena chahta hoon. Main tumhare bina adhoora hoon. Kaira, mujhe pata nahi kaise, lekin maine 22 din ek bada afraadh kiya hai... Plz mujhe ek mauka de do..."*

His breath became rapid, his heart racing, as the weight of his words pressed down on him. He could feel the intensity of the moment, as though everything he had ever wanted hinged on Kaira's answer. But all he had now were his memories and hopes, clinging to the idea that, one day, something could bring them back together.

And then, as if nothing had changed, Gautam smiled as he picked up the pen again, continuing his letter to Kaira, as if she was still by his side:

Dear Chotu Baba,

Aaj lunch mein kya khane waala hai? Mai ghar se khana le aau? Mangu bhai se baat hui, wo kya kar rahe hain? Chalo na, aaj kahin bahar chalte hain... I hope you're having a peaceful morning, and that your day is as beautiful as you are.

And just before you sleep, my dear, I want to say—Good night, Chotu Baba. Please so jaana, agar neend na aaye toh call me.

I love you to the moon and back, Chotu

I promise, kal se bohot achhe se padhai karunga.

Gautam's heart swelled as he finished the letter, each word soaked with emotion, his desire for reconciliation and love poured onto paper. But more than anything, he wanted Kaira to know, wherever she was, that he couldn't live without her. She was his everything, and without her, he was incomplete. Yet, despite all the pain, he held onto the hope that someday, something would bring them back together.

He would keep working on himself, keep growing, keep searching for the right job, and he would continue believing—because Kaira deserved the best, and he wanted to give her that.

Every day, he stared at her WhatsApp DP, with the believe that she might unclock him. Hoping that one day, Kaira would smile back at him, and they would find their way back to each other.

www.ingramcontent.com/pod-product-compliance
Lightning Source LLC
LaVergne TN
LVHW041129150826
845673LV00007B/2242

* 9 7 9 8 8 9 7 2 4 6 1 6 8 *